Mystery of the
Melting Snowman

Library of Congress Cataloging-in-Publication data

Heide, Florence Parry,
Mystery of the melting snowman.
Summary: The Spotlight Club detectives are involved in a new case concerning a
mysterious man and an iron dog.
[I. Mystery and detective stories] I. Heide,
Roxanne, joint author. II. Fleishman, Seymour, illus.
PZ7.H36Myf
[Fic] 74-16333
ISBN 0-8075-5378-6
Paperback edition: 978-0-8075-7705-9

10 9 8 7 6 5 4 3 2 1 BP 18 17 16 15 14 13

Illustrations by Seymour Fleishman

For information about Albert Whitman & Company,
visit our web site at www.albertwhitman.com.

Contents

Mystery of the Melting Snowman

FLORENCE PARRY HEIDE AND
ROXANNE HEIDE PIERCE

Albert Whitman & Company
Chicago, Illinois

CHAPTER 1
Shadows on the Snow

SOMETHING WAKENED JAY suddenly. He opened his eyes wide. Light was flashing onto his face through his bedroom window.

He sprang out of bed and ran over to the window. "The signal!" he whispered out loud. It was pitch dark between the flashes of light. Snow had started to fall.

It was Dexter, right next door, flashing a light from his own window. The signal was a special one for the Spotlight Club members. It meant *Come over now!* They never used the telephone late at night. Their parents had made that rule.

Jay ran back to his bed. He reached under it and grabbed his own flashlight. Leaning against the cold windowsill, he flashed one long flash and two short ones. That meant he'd be right over.

He threw on his clothes. He kept his flashlight with him and went as quietly as he could into his sister's room.

"Cindy!" he whispered. "It's the signal from Dexter."

Cindy was awake instantly.

"Let's hurry," whispered Jay. "I'll run over right now. You meet us. OK?"

Cindy nodded. She was already out of bed and reaching for her clothes.

Jay crept down the stairs. He grabbed his coat and scarf from the hook in the hall.

He let himself out of the front door very quietly and walked out on the porch. He ran down the steps and turned to go over to Dexter's.

A tall snowman stood in the yard. Just as Jay passed it he saw Dexter crouching on his porch. Dexter pointed. Jay looked. A tall figure dressed in a parka was moving quickly and quietly across the snow.

Jay stared after him. Dexter ran over to Jay.

"Hurry," whispered Dexter. "We've got to follow him. I'll explain later." The boys started to run across the snow. Except for a single street lamp swaying on the corner, there was no light anywhere.

Dexter and Jay ran to the next corner. There was no streetlight. There was no sound. They stood and peered into the darkness.

"We've lost him," said Dexter.

Suddenly they heard the sound of a car door slamming. Then an engine starting up. The car drove off without turning its headlights on.

"He's gone," sighed Dexter, taking off his misted glasses.

"Who was he?" asked Jay.

"I don't know," Dexter said. "But he was out in front of the Maxwells' house next door. He was taking their snowmen apart. I'd gone into the bathroom on that side of the house to get a drink of water. And there he was out in the Maxwells' yard. I kept watching. He smashed the snowmen to pieces! Then he started over to the snowman on our lawn. That's when I signaled you."

The boys started back to Dexter's house.

"What do you think he was doing?" asked Jay.

"I don't know," answered Dexter. "He must have been looking for something."

"Looking for something in a snowman?" asked Jay. Then he grabbed Dexter. "Look!" he whispered. "There he is."

"Where?" asked Dexter, looking around.

"Behind the snowman in your yard," said Jay, peering through the dark. Suddenly they both realized it was Cindy.

"Where were you?" she whispered. They ran up to her and explained quickly in hushed voices.

"He had to be looking for something," concluded Dexter.

"Maybe he doesn't like snowmen," said Cindy.

"He was looking for something, all right," said Jay. "But he didn't know exactly where to look. First he tried the snowmen that were in the Maxwells' yard."

"He didn't find anything there," said Cindy. "He was going to look in this snowman next." She tapped its stomach with her mitten.

Shadows on the Snow

They looked at the snowman from top to bottom.

"Let's take the snowman apart," said Cindy quickly. "Before he comes back."

"I'll try to dig it out from the back," said Jay. "The man won't see me that way. You two stand guard. Give the signal if you hear or see the car coming back."

"Maybe he'll park it somewhere else and walk," said Cindy. "We'll have to work fast."

Jay tried to make himself as small as possible behind the big snowman. He took a penknife from his jacket pocket. Carefully he dug at the snow, starting with the head.

He pushed his hand through the snow around the hole he had made. Nothing. Nothing but snow.

His fingers were so cold he could hardly move them. He blew on them for a minute. Then he started to dig out a hole in the middle part of the snowman.

A tree branch creaked above him and he jumped. He kept digging. Suddenly his fingers hit something. Something hard, harder than snow.

Jay drew his hand back quickly. He motioned to Dexter and Cindy. They ran over. "There's something in here," whispered Jay. "And it's mighty cold and hard." He blew on his fingers again.

Dexter reached in. "Wow," he said. "Cold is right. Let's dig it out."

"But we don't want him to come back and see us," said Cindy. "Let's take turns watching for his car."

It took a long time. They had to take most of the snowman apart. And then they were able to pull the object out.

"What is it?" asked Jay. Dexter brushed the snow off. They all stared.

It was a heavy iron dog, sitting on its haunches, with its paws against its chest. The iron jaws held an iron ball.

They stood looking at it. "I don't understand," whispered Cindy finally. "Who put it in the snowman? And why?"

"Let's put it back," said Dexter. "We don't know who it belongs to, but it doesn't belong to us. The man will come back and find us and—"

"No," insisted Jay. "Whoever came for it came sneaking. That means he was doing something wrong."

Shadows on the Snow

"Well, we're sneaking," said Cindy.

"We're detectives," said Jay.

"I know what to do," Dexter said quickly. "Let's take the iron dog in the house and stay up and watch. We can see who comes for it. Whoever it was might be stealing it. If he's on the level, he'll come back in the morning and ask about it. We should keep it safe until we know what it's all about."

"Right," agreed Jay. "Let's put the snowman back together just the way it was. Then there's nothing to suspect. Maybe the man will come back and try to find the dog. That way we can see him and find out what he's up to."

In a few minutes the snowman was as good as new.

Dexter took the iron dog. "I'll carry it into the house," he said. "I've got gloves."

Jay and Cindy were right behind him. Cindy turned to look at the snowman as they shut the door. It looked just as it had before.

Dexter set the iron dog down in the front hall. "Why was the dog in the snowman?" he muttered.

"He'll come back to get it," Jay said. "We'll have to stay here all night and take turns watching."

"What will he do when he finds it's gone?" wondered Cindy out loud. The boys shrugged.

"If we're going to stay here for the night," said Jay, "we'll have to let Mom know where we are."

"I'll go over and leave a note," Cindy offered. "I have to get my notebook anyway. I can't think without it."

8

Shadows on the Snow

"Your notebook!" exploded Jay. "It's the middle of the night, and we have a mystery and a dog and some stranger who's breaking up snowmen out there somewhere, and you think about your notebook."

"You'll be glad I've got it," said Cindy. "I can keep track of every clue and write down questions as we think of them." She stood for a moment looking out at the snow. Was the stranger waiting and watching out there?

"I'll walk over with you," said Jay.

"I'm not afraid," lied Cindy.

"I know. But I'm going with you anyway," answered Jay.

In a few minutes they were back. They had left a note for Mrs. Temple, and Cindy had her notebook. They had seen no one.

Dexter had waited and watched. When they came in, he pulled three sleeping bags from the closet under the stairs. "We can take turns staying awake and watching," he said. "The watcher can sit on the radiator and look out the window. If the lights are off in here, no one can see in."

"We can get a good look at him if he comes back," said Jay. "And we can follow him and get a good look at his car. Maybe we'll find out just who he is and what he wants."

Cindy took her notebook. "Let's figure out what we know while we're all wide awake."

"You mean, what we *don't* know," said Dexter.

"Here's what we know so far," Cindy said. "An iron dog was hidden in the snowman. Someone came to get it. Let's call him Mr. X, the way we always do when we're working on a mystery." She wrote busily, reading out loud as she wrote:

Query: Why was Mr. X pulling the snowmen apart?

Answer: He was looking for something.

Query: What was he looking for?

Answer: The iron dog.

Query: What do we know about Mr. X?

Answer: a) He's tall.

b) He's wearing a parka with a hood.

c) He doesn't want to be seen, therefore

he is probably doing something wrong. For example, taking the dog, which doesn't belong to him.

d) He left in a car and didn't turn the headlights on, so he didn't want to be seen leaving.

Cindy tapped her pencil. "Where was his car parked?" she asked.

"Just at the end of the street," said Jay. "There's a broken water main, and this street is blocked off. His car was right behind the barricade."

"Whoever he is, he'll be back," Dexter said, pulling his glasses down on his nose.

Cindy reached over and touched the iron dog. "What's so important about this dog? Why does Mr. X want to get it? Who put it there? What's it all about?"

"What on earth is going on?" asked a voice from the top of the stairs. It was Dexter's sister Anne.

"We just found this dog," said Dexter.

"Someone was knocking the snowmen down," explained Jay.

"The boys chased him and lost him," added Cindy.

Anne shook her head. "I don't mind mysteries. But I mind mysteries in the middle of the night. When I heard you talking I thought you were burglars until I realized burglars don't stand around talking. They start burgling. I just guessed it was you three. My ESP told me."

She yawned. "If Dad and Mom hear you, you're in trouble," she said. "You know how parents are. They think people should sleep at night and solve mysteries during the day." She turned to go back to her room.

Dexter turned to Jay and Cindy. "She's right about our folks getting mad if they hear us," he whispered. "Let's keep it quiet. I'll take first watch. You two get some sleep."

"Wake me when you get sleepy, Dex," said Jay. "I'll take the next watch."

Dexter nodded. He sat on the radiator cover, his sleeping bag wrapped around him. His face was cold leaning against the window, but the rest of him was warm from the radiator. He pulled his glasses down on his nose and stared out into the night.

Shadows on the Snow

The street lamp swayed, making the shadow of the snowman lean first one way and then another. A gust of wind caught the powdery snow on the ground and swished it high up in the air. Dexter looked up and down the street. He didn't see a thing. He yawned and shifted his position.

Was it the snowman's shadow that was moving? Or someone else's? Dexter squinted through his glasses.

Suddenly he sat up straight. "Psssst!" he whispered to Jay and Cindy. "Wake up! He's back!"

CHAPTER 2
Who and Why?

THE THREE DETECTIVES pushed their faces against the cold window. A tall figure in a hooded parka was slowly walking around the big snowman. The hood shielded his face from view.

As the Spotlighters watched, the man started to dig into the middle of the snowman. He reached in, then he drew himself up and looked around. Suddenly he started to knock the snowman down.

"He's really mad," whispered Jay.

"What will he do when he can't find it?" Cindy whispered back.

"When he knows the iron dog isn't in there, he'll

Who and Why?

leave," said Dexter. "Let's be ready to follow him. We can at least get a look at his car. Maybe we can trace him from that."

In a moment the snowman had been completely destroyed.

"Be ready to grab your jackets and run after him," whispered Jay. "But we have to be quiet about it. If he hears us, he'll know we're following him, and he'll know we have the dog."

"What would he do to us?" asked Cindy, shivering.

"You can stay here, Cindy, if you want to," said Dexter.

"Not me," she whispered.

The tall figure stood and stared around him. The Spotlighters ducked out of sight as he turned to look at the house.

When they carefully edged their faces up again, he was walking toward the barricade at the end of the street.

"Hurry," said Jay. They threw on their jackets and rushed to the front door. "Easy does it," whispered Dexter. He opened the door a crack. A blast of cold air hit their faces. They shivered and peered out into the dark. It took a moment to spot him again.

"He's started over to his car," whispered Dexter.

Dexter, Cindy, and Jay walked quickly over the snow toward the street. In a moment they reached the barricade. Fresh tire tracks in the snow told them he had gone.

"He's gone!" said Jay. "He really moved fast!"

They walked back to Dexter's.

"He's gone, and we don't know one single thing," wailed Cindy as they hung their jackets on hooks in the hall.

She got out her notebook. "I have my notebook, but I don't know what to write," she said. "We don't know who he is or why he wanted the iron dog. Or anything."

"He came back for it," said Jay. "He's still tall and he's still wearing a parka. He knocked down our snowman looking for something. And he left in the car again. End of clues!"

"Your brain must be frozen," said Dexter. "It isn't the end. It's just the beginning! When was that snowman built?"

"Yesterday afternoon," said Jay, scratching his head.

"Right," said Dexter. "While you and I were doing your paper route."

Who and Why?

Cindy interrupted excitedly. "The little Maxwell kids were building it. I was watching them for Mrs. Maxwell while she went to market. I helped them with the bottom snowball. We started it in their yard and rolled it into yours, Dexter. And then Mrs. Maxwell came back and I remembered I'd promised Mom that I'd pare the carrots and peel the potatoes. And then when I came out again, about an hour later, the snowman was finished!"

She stared at the iron dog. "Someone helped the Maxwell children with that snowman. I'm sure of it. And that means—that means whoever hid the iron dog! Nobody was around but the kids. He just rolled the dog into the middle snowball."

"And planned to come back later," Dexter added.

"So we ask the Maxwell kids who helped them and we've found Mr. X," said Jay slowly.

Cindy wrote *Plans* at the top of a new page in her notebook. "I suppose we can't go over and ask them now?" she asked.

"Almost, but not quite," grinned Dexter. "They're up at the crack of dawn every day. I know. I live next door."

"Then it's settled," said Cindy, closing her notebook. "The Maxwell house is the first stop tomorrow morning. We'd better get some sleep now."

The three detectives arranged their sleeping bags and were asleep within minutes.

Cindy was the first to waken. She crawled out of her sleeping bag and looked through the window. There were only piles of trampled snow in the yard. Last night's adventure was no dream.

"We've got to talk to the Maxwell kids," she whispered loudly to waken Jay and Dexter.

Half awake, the boys muttered to each other, "Got to do it. Talk to the Maxwell kids."

"Here," Cindy said, "let me roll up the sleeping bags. Let's get started."

"I hope I wake up pretty soon," said Jay.

"I have an awful time being a detective on an empty stomach," said Dexter. "Let's have breakfast first."

They fixed breakfast and left the house munching apples. The two little Maxwell children were already coming outside.

Amy smiled up at Cindy and picked up some snow.

Who and Why?

"Making more snowmen?" asked Cindy.

"They're all gone," cried Amy. "They melted and melted flat."

"They didn't melt," Randy said, frowning. "Somebody smashed them all up. Bang! Crash! Pow!"

"How do you know?" Dexter asked. "Did you see someone do that?"

Randy shuffled his feet in the snow. "No. I just know they didn't melt, that's all. It's too cold."

"We'll build another big snowman later," promised Cindy.

"Now-now-now-now!" shouted Amy. She sat down on the snow and started humming to herself.

Cindy turned to Randy. "Do you remember yesterday when I helped you build the bottom of the snowman?"

"Sure," Randy said.

"Then I had to leave, remember?"

"Sure," Randy said again.

"Did someone else come and help you with the snowman?" Cindy asked.

Amy nodded. "Oh, yes, and he had two Amys in

his eyes. Two Amys, two Amys!" she said, patting the snow around her.

"Two what?" asked Cindy. Amy didn't make any sense.

"Two Amys," cried Amy again.

Randy was throwing a snowball up in the air and catching it.

"Who helped you with the snowman, Randy?" Cindy asked him again.

"Some man," Randy said. "He was nice. He told us to go in the house and get a carrot for the nose." He tossed his snowball in the air and watched it splat on the ground. "So Amy and I went in the

Who and Why?

back door and waited for Mom to get us a carrot for the nose."

Cindy thought quickly. That was when the man must have put the dog in the snowman.

"What did he look like, Randy?" asked Cindy.

"He was nice," Randy said.

Amy had come up behind Randy and was tugging on his jacket. "Gotcha last!" she squealed, and started running. Randy shouted after Amy, "Oh no, I'll get you last." He ran after her. They both disappeared behind the house.

"He sent them in the house for a carrot," said Jay. "That's when he rolled the dog into the snowman."

"Let's talk to the kids again," Dexter said. "Amy doesn't make sense, she's too little. But maybe we can find out more from Randy."

"All we know so far is that a tall man in a parka was looking for the iron dog in the snowman," sighed Cindy. "A tall man in a parka."

Dexter stared behind Cindy. "Here comes a man now," he said. "A tall man in a parka!"

CHAPTER 3
Watching and Waiting

CINDY TURNED AROUND and faced a young man with blond hair. He was striding toward them. Jay was right—he was tall. And he was wearing a parka. The hood was down.

He was wearing large mirror sunglasses, and he was carrying a small metal box under his arm. He shifted it to the other arm, and something inside the box clanked. His glasses turned in the direction of the three detectives.

"Nice morning!" he said.

"Sure is," said Dexter.

Cindy looked at the man's face. She saw herself

reflected in his glasses—two blue jackets, two Cindys. Her thoughts raced. What was it that Amy had said? She saw two Amys in his eyes? Of course! This was the man who had helped Amy and Randy with the snowman! It must be.

Cindy couldn't tell whether his eyes were looking at her or at Dexter or Jay or what. The mirror glasses were like a mask.

The young man looked at the Maxwells' house. Then at the Tates'. Then at the Temples'. At least, thought Cindy, he turned his head in those directions. With those glasses you couldn't tell. Anybody who wore glasses like that must have shifty eyes, she decided.

Amy and Randy came running around the side of the house. "I'm a big snowman and I'm going to get you!" shouted Randy. Amy squealed and ran toward Cindy.

At that moment the young man quickly pulled his glasses off and put them in his pocket.

Cindy stared. Why would he do that? Unless he thought Amy was going to recognize his glasses?

"I got you!" shouted Randy, and Amy squealed

some more. Cindy glanced down at Amy. She was too excited with their game to notice the young man. Randy looked up at him and cocked his head to one side. Then he started to chase Amy again. The young man turned and walked quickly across the street.

"He's the one," whispered Cindy as soon as he was out of earshot.

Jay laughed. "Just because he's wearing a parka? And he's tall?"

"Not just that," said Cindy quickly. "He was wearing mirror sunglasses. Amy said she saw two Amys in his eyes, remember? Well, when Amy was running toward us just now, he took his glasses off in a hurry. He didn't want Amy and Randy to recognize him."

Dexter whistled. "Let's follow him," he said.

"Wait," said Cindy. "We don't want him to guess that we have the iron dog."

"I wonder what was in that metal box he was carrying," mused Dexter.

"Why did he steal the dog in the first place?" asked Jay. "Who really owns it?"

"We don't know for sure that he stole it," said

Watching and Waiting

Dexter. "Remember Mr. Hooley's Rule. We have to *prove* everything." Amy and Randy were back.

"Was the man who was just here the man who helped you with the snowman yesterday?" Cindy asked Randy.

Randy shook his head. "The man that helped us had funny glasses." He turned around and started chasing Amy again.

The three detectives watched as the man stopped in front of the red house on the corner.

"He's going up to that house," Jay said.

Sure enough, the stranger walked up the porch steps and rang the doorbell. A minute later the door opened, and he walked inside.

"At least we know where he is," said Cindy.

"We've got to keep an eye on him."

"I've got it," said Jay. "You and I can shovel the walk for Mr. Mulberry, Dex. His house is right across the street from the red house. That way we can watch the house without looking suspicious. And besides, Mr. Mulberry shouldn't be shoveling snow anyway. OK?"

"Sounds swell," said Dexter. "How about you, Cindy?"

"I'll poke around here and see if I can find anything in the snow," she said. "Any clue."

The boys ran around to the garage to get the snow shovels, then off for the Mulberrys' house.

Amy and Randy came running over to Cindy. "Help us, Cindy, help us!" Amy cried.

"I can't make a big snowman now, but I'll make you some little ones," said Cindy. She knelt down in the snow. She made five tiny snowmen.

Just as Cindy turned over another little pile of snow, she caught a glimpse of something bright orange. Her fingers closed over several strands of wool fringe and she pulled. It was a long orange scarf.

"The snowman's scarf!" cried Amy. "The man gave it to us."

"You mean the man who helped you wore this scarf?" asked Cindy.

Amy nodded and nodded.

Cindy put the scarf in her pocket. If this is Mr. X's scarf, it almost proves he was the one who put the dog in the snowman, she thought.

Watching and Waiting

Just then Cindy heard Anne calling from the porch. "Oh, there you are, Cindy. I don't know who's to blame for my stubbed toe, you or this silly creature. What is it, anyway? It must be a doorstop to a castle door or something."

"Wait!" Cindy cried. "I'll be right there." She hoped nobody had heard Anne. Or had seen her standing on the porch holding the iron dog.

Cindy ran up to her. "It's a very important part of our mystery. If anyone comes around asking about it, you've never heard about the iron dog."

"What dog?" asked Anne, winking.

Cindy laughed and took the iron dog. "Thanks," she said. "I'll tell you more about the mystery later." She put the dog under her coat and ran across Dexter's yard to her own yard.

She ran into the house. "Hi, Mom," she called, setting the dog down on the floor of the living room. It was pretty heavy.

Mrs. Temple called from upstairs. "I just got up and I found your note. What were you doing over at the Tates' in the middle of the night?"

"We didn't wake you up, did we?" asked Cindy, running upstairs.

"Oh, no," Mrs. Temple said. "I had my special little cotton balls in my ears. I was sure that you three would find some kind of mystery before Christmas vacation is over—and it's almost over."

Cindy walked into her mother's bedroom. Mrs. Temple was dressed and was brushing her hair.

"We did find a mystery, Mom," Cindy said. "A real one. I'll tell you about it later. I've got to go outside again and help Jay and Dexter spy. Do you want me to do anything first?"

Watching and Waiting

"Nothing," smiled Mrs. Temple. "I'm going to curl up downstairs with a book. It's heaven not thinking about going to work today. Even though I do love my job. You're in the clear for the day."

"Thanks, Mom!" Cindy said. She ran downstairs to get the iron dog. She carried it upstairs to her room. Why was it so important? She turned the animal around and around and looked at it from all sides. She turned it upside down. Then she pushed it out of sight, under her bed. It would be safe there.

When Cindy came downstairs, Mrs. Temple was carrying a cup of coffee into the living room.

"I'm going to sit here curled up like a kitten all morning," she said, smiling. "I have a stack of beautiful books from the library. And today the Tates are taking me to Chicago and then to dinner and a movie. I have nothing to do but spoil myself. You don't mind having TV dinners this one night, do you?"

Cindy smiled. "I like them better than TV."

"Oh, and do have Dexter over too. Anne is going with us, and there won't be anyone over there either."

"OK," Cindy said, taking her mittens off the radiator. "Mom, do you know who lives in that big old red house across the street? The one up at the corner."

Mrs. Temple sipped her coffee. "Never ask a working mother anything about neighbors," she said. "I hear nothing, I see nothing, I know nothing. But that house changes hands a lot. I used to know who lived there five or six years ago, but I've lost track."

Cindy laughed. "Well, I'm rushing off to solve a big mystery, Mom. See you later."

As Cindy walked down the porch steps she saw a familiar face and heard a familiar voice. It was Mrs. Selma Peabody, the neighborhood gossip. "Oh, no," groaned Cindy to herself.

"I was going to drive my car over to the sale," said Mrs. Peabody. "But with the street torn up I had to leave my car there behind the barricade. I'll probably catch my death."

"What sale?" Cindy asked, curious.

"The one up there at the corner in the red house,"

Watching and Waiting

Mrs. Peabody said. "Imagine, having a sale. Strangers tramping through your house, pawing things."

Cindy thought quickly. A sale in the red house. That's where the man in the parka had gone. If there was a sale, then anyone could go. The Spotlighters could go. She could walk right in with Jay and Dexter and spy on Mr. X.

Cindy quickened her pace. Surely now they could find out more about the iron dog and Mr. X, the man with the mirror sunglasses.

"Did they put an ad in the paper?" Cindy asked Mrs. Peabody. She was sure that she would have seen it if anyone had—she always read everything in the newspaper.

Mrs. Peabody shook her head. "There was a sign in the bakery window this morning. 'Sale of Household Goods, Neighbors and Friends Welcome,' it said. And it gave that address. And the funny thing is that it's old Mrs. Wellington's house. And she hasn't even been living there. Not for weeks, mind you. Where is she? And who's selling her things? That's what I'd like to know, and that's what I'm going to find out."

She leaned closer to Cindy and said, "There's something funny going on. Otherwise, why would they be selling her things?" Mrs. Peabody sniffed and crossed the street to the red house.

Cindy could see that Jay and Dexter were still shoveling the Mulberrys' walk. She ran over to them. "Did you see anything suspicious?" she asked.

"Yes," said Jay. "That's the third lady who's walked into the house. But we haven't seen a sign of Mr. X."

"It's a sale," Cindy said quickly. "Mrs. Peabody said there was a sign in the bakery this morning. Household goods. She said the house belonged to Mrs. Wellington. Mrs. Peabody thinks it's funny that someone is selling Mrs. Wellington's things. But Mrs. Peabody thinks everything is funny."

"Let's go," said Dexter.

"OK, as soon as we finish the driveway," Jay said. "We can't stop now or Mr. Mulberry will finish it."

Dexter asked, "Did you find any clues over there in the snow, Cindy?"

"I did find something," Cindy said, patting her bulging pocket. "An orange scarf. Amy said the man gave it to her. I'm going over to the red house now and see what I can find out."

"We'll be over as soon as we can," said Jay.

"Good," Cindy said. "See you there." She ran across the street and up the porch steps of the house Mr. X had entered.

CHAPTER 4
Inside the Red House

CINDY RANG THE doorbell. Would the man with the mirror glasses open the door?

She waited only a moment. The door opened and Cindy looked into the face of a small, pretty young woman with blond hair. She was about as tall as Cindy.

"How do you do?" she said. "I don't know you, but I'm so pleased that you came for the sale. My name is Jenny Mayflower."

"I'm Cindy Temple," said Cindy. "I live just across the street a couple of houses down."

"I'm sorry that I know so few of the neighbors," said Jenny Mayflower. "That's what happens when you're busy."

Inside the Red House

"That's just what my mother says," agreed Cindy. She glanced around. The young man with the mirror sunglasses was nowhere to be seen.

There was a desk on the left side of the front door, a pad of paper on the desk. Beautiful dishes and goblets and silver were on tables in the next room.

Two women were walking around the dining room table looking at the things spread out on it. Mrs. Peabody was in the living room, picking up each item, examining it, and looking at the price marked on it.

"Are you selling everything here?" Cindy asked Jenny Mayflower.

"As much as we can!" laughed Jenny. "If you can pick it up, you can buy it. You don't have to buy a thing, you know, but you are welcome to look around all you like. If you find something you want, my fiancé is in charge of the money part of things. He's much better at that than I am. He's upstairs right now, finding light bulbs."

Cindy was thinking about what Mrs. Peabody had told her. That it was funny someone was selling all of Mrs. Wellington's things.

"Do you live here?" she asked Jenny.

"I've been living here with Mrs. Melanie Wellington," Jenny answered. "I've been her secretary and companion. But I'm getting married in three days. We're moving into a tiny apartment near Chicago." She smiled and looked around the house. "I've loved it here, and I'll really miss Mrs. Wellington."

"Doesn't she live here anymore?" asked Cindy.

"No, she lives on the other side of town. In a lovely place called the North Star."

Cindy made a mental note of the name.

"Tonight I'm going to meet Tom's parents for the very first time," Jenny confided. "They're flying in from Arizona to be at the wedding. We're meeting their plane. Oh, I hope they like me!"

"They will," Cindy assured her.

"And then we'll see Mrs. Wellington tonight," Jenny added. "She's been so kind. And she'll want to meet Tom's parents."

Now that she had met Jenny, Cindy was sorry Jenny was leaving the neighborhood so soon. It would have been fun to have a young friendly neighbor like this.

Inside the Red House

Jenny looked past Cindy. Her smile grew even wider. "And here's the light bulb expert," she said. "Tom, I want you to meet one of our neighbors."

Cindy turned around. It was the young man in the mirror sunglasses, except he wasn't wearing them now. Jenny put her arm through Tom's and said, "Cindy, this is Tom Foster, my almost husband. Tom, this is my new friend, Cindy Temple."

Tom looked down at Cindy. "Any friend of Jenny's is a friend of mine," he grinned. His smile was a wide, friendly one, like Jenny's.

Did he recognize Cindy? Her thoughts raced. This was the man that Jenny Mayflower was going to marry in three days. And this was the man who had hidden the iron dog in the snowman. Or had he? Cindy remembered Mr. Hooley's Rule. She had to have proof.

Tom walked to the desk that Cindy had noticed when she had come in. He reached into a drawer and brought out a metal box. It was the one he had been carrying when Cindy first saw him.

Tom raised his eyebrows. "This metal box will be jammed with money by the end of the day. Lucky

I'm in charge of things. You'd give everything away for nothing!" He chuckled.

Cindy was trying to sort out her thoughts. The Maxwell children said a nice man had helped them with the snowman. He wore mirror sunglasses. He had sent them in the house to get a carrot, and he gave them an orange scarf for the snowman. Cindy reached in her bulging jacket pocket and felt the damp scarf. She pulled it out.

"We found this in the snow this morning," Cindy said. "Does it belong to anybody here?"

Tom blushed bright red. He started to doodle on the pad in front of him.

Jenny reached for the scarf. "Why, it's yours, Tom!" she exclaimed. "You told me you'd lost it ages and ages ago!"

Just then the doorbell rang. Three more ladies came in. They started to talk to Jenny. Cindy walked thoughtfully into the dining room. Why had Tom told Jenny that he had lost the scarf long ago?

Cindy pretended to look at some cups and saucers that were on a table in the dining room. She wanted

to stay near enough to hear anything important Tom said.

Cindy waited and watched, moving around the downstairs pretending to look at the objects for sale.

Jenny went upstairs. She came down with her coat on. She was carrying a length of wide blue ribbon. When she saw Cindy, she winked.

Cindy walked over to her, and Jenny explained, "I'm going to tie this ribbon across the stairway. Some of these ladies are so curious they'll want to see what the rest of the house looks like."

Cindy helped her tie the ribbon across the stairs.

"Thanks a jillion," said Jenny. "I've got to run. I'm spending the rest of the day at the new apartment. Workmen are bringing the stove and the refrigerator and the new furniture—everything. And I've just got to be there."

Jenny walked over to Tom. Cindy followed. "And you, poor darling," Jenny said, ruffling Tom's hair, "you're going to be left holding the bag."

"I'll be glad to get rid of you," smiled Tom.

"Turn everyone out by three thirty, remember,"

said Jenny. "Lock up the house and turn off the lights. And come pick me up at the apartment. The furniture will all be there by then. And we'll have plenty of time to get to the airport to meet your mom and dad. I can't wait!"

"I'm sure they're even more excited than you are," said Tom. They smiled at each other with their wide, friendly smiles.

Jenny started to open the front door. Then she turned back and groaned and made a face. "My mind is absolutely going, going, gone. That's what I get for being so excited about a little thing like a wedding. Yesterday I forgot my car keys and had to come all the way back for them. And now I forgot to take that ugly vase out of my car. I don't want to drag it all the way into Chicago. And we could probably sell it here for five dollars."

"What ugly vase?" asked Tom.

"That big old brown thing with the handles that look like ears. I took it by mistake yesterday. I thought that doorstop was in the box. Then when I opened it I realized I had the wrong box. I don't know how it happened. Both boxes are the same size. I guess I just picked the wrong one."

Jenny turned to Cindy. "Could you walk with me back to my car and get the dreadful thing, Cindy? And bring it back here to Tom?"

"Sure," said Cindy. She hoped the boys would come over to watch Tom while she was gone. If he had stolen the iron dog he might steal something else. If, if, if, thought Cindy miserably. Everything was an *if*.

"It's such a headache having the end of the street shut off. But we ought to be back to normal by tomorrow," said Jenny. "Cindy, are you sure you don't mind coming along for the package?"

Cindy grinned. "I'm sure."

Jenny and Cindy walked down the steps of the house. Cindy glanced across the street. Jay and Dexter were talking to Mr. Mulberry. But they had one eye on the house. When they saw Cindy they waved. Cindy waved back. "I'll be right back!" she called. She knew they would go over to Mrs. Wellington's house to cover Tom Foster.

Cindy walked alongside Jenny toward her car. Did

Inside the Red House

Jenny know anything about the iron dog? Cindy wondered. About Tom's hiding it?

Cindy pointed across the street. "Someone broke all the snowmen last night," she said, watching Jenny. Jenny said nothing.

She led the way to her car. It was a little white sports car, dusted with snow. "White on white!" laughed Jenny.

Cindy helped her brush the snow from the windshield and the windows. As she did, she noted a green car with a bent fender parked right behind Jenny's car.

Jenny unlocked her car door and reached into the back seat. "Here it is, the ugliest of all vases," she said. She lifted out a big package. "Take this hideous thing back to the house, please. Maybe someone will buy it. Someone who can't see very well."

Cindy took the package and waved as Jenny drove away. She turned and started to walk back toward the house. Jay and Dexter were walking up the steps. Good. They'd watch Tom. And she could tell them everything she had discovered.

The wind was blowing in Cindy's face. She turned around so that she could walk backward.

Suddenly she stopped and stared, her heart pounding. There was someone—a man—hiding in the green car with the bent fender. As she watched he started to sit up. He had been crouching in the front seat!

CHAPTER 5
The Man in Black

THE MAN GOT out of the green car and slammed the door. He was tall and wore a long black coat. His hat was black and had a wide rim that came low over his forehead.

He looked up and stared at Cindy. Then his eyes went to the package she was holding. He started to walk toward her. His bushy black eyebrows met above a long thin nose. His eyes were black, and they narrowed as he came nearer.

Cindy stood still, facing him. He nodded at the package. "What's that?" he asked.

Cindy swallowed. What business was it of his? "It's

a package of Jenny Mayflower's," she said quickly. "I'm taking it to the house."

The man in black made a sound. It might have been a laugh, but he wasn't even smiling.

"Jenny Mayflower's, is it?" he asked.

Cindy nodded. She turned around and started toward the red house again.

"Jenny Mayflower's package, Jenny Mayflower's house, eh?" he said. He was beside her. He spoke quickly. "Look, I have reason to believe the package you carry contains stolen property."

Cindy's heart thudded. "What do you mean? It's just an old vase."

"We'll soon see. Hand it here." He reached over for the package.

Cindy drew away.

"You have to trust me," he said urgently. "How well do you know Jenny Mayflower?"

Cindy gulped. "I just met her today for the first time. And she wanted someone to carry this package from her car to the house. That's all."

The Man in Black

His eyebrows drew close together. "You only just met her today? Are you sure?"

"Of course I'm sure," said Cindy.

The man pulled at his chin. "Maybe you're in on it too, for all I know."

"In on what?" gasped Cindy. Her thoughts raced. It must have something to do with the iron dog.

"You don't know what's going on," said the man in black, glancing again at the package in Cindy's arms. "She's using you. That's stolen. Jenny Mayflower stole it. She thought if you carried it no one would trace it to her."

Suddenly Cindy was sure the man in black thought the iron dog was in this package.

"This isn't it!" she said without thinking. She bit her tongue. "I mean, it couldn't be stolen or anything. And Jenny's so nice. And why would she steal an old vase, anyway?"

Cindy started to run toward the red house. How dare this man accuse Jenny of stealing! She started up the steps. The man in black was right beside her. "Just hand me the package, young lady!" he said in a low whisper.

"But I told Jenny I'd take it in and give it to Tom," said Cindy. She was all mixed up. Who was to be trusted? Tom? Jenny? And who was this strange man? She couldn't think. And she was frightened.

She ran up the steps and opened the front door. She was sure the man in black was going to grab the box and run with it. But he only followed her up to the door.

"You'll see," he whispered under his breath. "You'll see I'm right. But in the meantime you must not tell anyone what I've told you. If Jenny Mayflower knows she is suspected of stealing she will run away."

The Man in Black

Cindy opened the door of the house and walked in. The man in black slipped into the house behind her.

Tom was standing at the table, talking to two ladies. One was Selma Peabody. The boys were nowhere in sight. They must be here somewhere, thought Cindy. She was going to need them.

"Here's the vase," she said, handing the package to Tom.

"A vase!" exclaimed Mrs. Peabody. "Let's see it. A vase is just what I need."

"Is it for sale?" asked the other lady.

"You bet," said Tom. "Everything here is for sale except the people." He picked up the box and started to open it.

The man in black cleared his throat. Cindy glanced over her shoulder at him. He had taken off his hat. He had black shiny hair combed straight back off a high forehead. His forehead was beaded with perspiration.

Tom lifted the object clear of the box. It was indeed a very ugly vase. The man in black sucked in his breath. Cindy knew he had expected it to be the iron dog. She knew it.

"Oh, it's lovely," said Mrs. Peabody. "How much is it?"

Tom considered. "You may have it for three dollars, madam," he said.

"I'll take it," said Mrs. Peabody, "although it probably isn't worth more than ten cents."

The man in black edged closer to Cindy. "Say nothing of our conversation until I have spoken with you again," he whispered. "Remember. Nothing."

She stared at him. He turned on his heel and walked into the living room. His eyes took in the entire room.

There was a room beyond that, and he walked in. His eyes searched the room. He was looking for the iron dog. Cindy knew it, she knew it. Or did she? She didn't know what to think. She had to have more facts first.

Where were the boys? Cindy glanced around quickly. On the other side of the dining room on the far end of the house was a porch. A glassed-in porch with a lot of plants. Sort of like a greenhouse, she decided. And there was Dexter. He was leaning over a plant and reading a sign on it.

The Man in Black

She had to be sure that the man in black did not leave the house. But he probably wouldn't go until he had talked to her again. And she had to talk to Jay and Dexter.

She walked quickly over to the porch. Dexter looked up and grinned. Once she was out on the porch she could see that Jay was there too.

"Quick," Cindy said in a low voice. "I've got to talk to you. There's a man in black who came in when I did. He thought the box I was carrying held the iron dog. At least I think he did. But it was an old ugly vase, just the way Jenny Mayflower had said. Anyway, he said Jenny had stolen whatever was in the package." She stopped to catch her breath.

"Slow down, slow down," said Jay. "Who's Jenny Mayflower? Why did the man in black think she had stolen something? What's going on? Start at the beginning."

Cindy quickly told them about meeting Jenny. About Jenny and Tom. About the scarf. "But I'm sure that Tom couldn't have been doing anything wrong when he hid the iron dog in the snowman," she said.

"He may have been hiding it from someone. Maybe from this man in black!" She bit her lip. "We've got to find out something more. We can't have him going around saying that Jenny Mayflower is a thief!"

Dexter looked behind Cindy. "The man in black is in the dining room," he said.

Cindy turned around. As she watched, the man looked quickly around the room. Then he silently pushed open the swinging door and walked into the kitchen. It must be the kitchen, thought Cindy, right next to the dining room, and with a swinging door.

"I'm going in there and ask him what he's talking about," announced Cindy. "I'll just find out everything I can." The boys started to argue with her, but she was already halfway across the room. Her heart thudded. What was she going to say to the man in black?

Cindy pushed open the swinging door. She walked into the kitchen.

It was empty.

Where had he gone? The back door! Of course! He had got away after all. She ran over to the door and threw it open. There was fresh snow on the steps.

The Man in Black

No one had gone in or out of the door that day. She breathed a sigh of relief.

But where was he? She looked around the kitchen. In addition to the back door to the outside there were two other doors. Would he be hiding in a closet? Why? Was he looking for the iron dog in the closets? She smiled grimly to herself. He'd never find it, not if he looked for a million years. He'd never guess it was under Cindy Temple's bed!

She listened again. And this time she was sure she heard a creaking. She stood for a moment in front of the door, and then she took a deep breath and flung it open.

It wasn't a closet after all. It was a door to steps that led upstairs. Cindy peered up the dark passageway, trying to see to the top. She put one foot on the bottom step and listened. What right had the man in black to sneak around Jenny's house? She took another step up, then another. There was no railing to hold onto. The steps were steep and curving.

Slowly she climbed up. One of the steps creaked noisily. She stopped and held her breath. There was no sound from upstairs, only the murmuring of voices from below.

She came to the curve in the stairway and tried to look beyond the top step. It was too dark to see anything. She shivered. Maybe she should go back down and get the boys. But she had to find out what the man in black was doing. He was probably trying to steal something—and then he'd blame Jenny! Of course! Just thinking about it made Cindy angry.

She reached the top step and stared ahead. There was a long hallway. It was too dark to see what was at the end of it from where she stood. There was only a faint light coming from an open door. She started to walk slowly down the hall. There were several other doors, all of them closed.

She came to the one door ajar and glanced inside. Strange—she saw vases filled with flowers. The room looked ready for guests. But she tiptoed quickly past.

And suddenly she saw that someone was standing at the end of the long dark hall. She caught her breath. It looked like Jenny.

The Man in Black

Cindy started forward. The figure at the end of the hall started forward at the same instant.

"Jenny?" whispered Cindy. She stood still, waiting for an answer. The figure had stopped too. There was no sound, no answer.

Was it Jenny? She had to find out. She walked quickly and silently toward the figure. The figure walked toward her. And suddenly Cindy was face to face with the other person. She was staring into her own eyes. A mirror! It was framed in dark brown wood and was fastened to the door. At the top of the glass was etched an owl with outstretched wings.

And then suddenly Cindy heard a noise to her right. She turned her head. The doorknob of the closed door was turning slowly.

What was behind that door? The man in black—it must be. With wide eyes Cindy stared. She couldn't take her eyes off the turning doorknob.

The door opened slowly toward Cindy. She was glued to the spot. It was the man in black. He stared down at her. His black eyes under his bushy black eyebrows seemed to bore right through her. He grabbed her arm. Cindy tried to pull loose, but his long thin fingers gripped tightly. She opened her mouth to call for help.

"Wait!" he whispered urgently. "You don't understand! I'm a detective!"

CHAPTER 6
A Detective!

"YOU'RE A DETECTIVE!" gasped Cindy.

"No wonder you suspected me," said the man in black. "Of course you thought I was acting in a very suspicious manner. How were you to know? And I couldn't explain. I was afraid you might tell someone."

Cindy swallowed. "I'm sorry. I just didn't realize—"

The man interrupted. "I feel I can trust you. I feel I can trust you to cooperate with our investigation." His black eyes peered at her. "I can, can't I? I can trust you?"

She nodded.

"My name is Alex Baxter. I've been working on

this case for some time. In fact, there are several men assigned to the case. It is that important. And we are finally nearing the end. We have the break we've been looking for." He paused.

"Maybe we can help you," Cindy said quickly. "My name's Cindy Temple. I live just across the street. My brother and our next-door neighbor and I have a detective club. The boys are downstairs now. We've solved a lot of mysteries."

"A detective club!" exclaimed Alex Baxter. His eyes gleamed. "Perfect! I'll have to talk to all of you right now. Privately. We can't let Tom Foster overhear us. I think you may be helpful. Yes, most helpful."

Cindy thought fast. Then Tom Foster was in on it after all, in on whatever was happening.

Alex Baxter jerked his head toward the back stairway. "I'll meet you and your detective club out on that porch where all the plants are. Hurry! We have no time to lose."

Cindy turned and ran quickly down the hall to the back stairway. She crept down the steps. She listened at the door before she opened it into the kitchen.

A Detective!

Everything was quiet except for the hum of voices in the rest of the house.

She slipped noiselessly into the kitchen. The boys were not in sight. But she found Jay in the study on the other side of the living room. "Where's Dexter?" she asked in a whisper. "We've got to have a meeting—fast!"

"What's up?" asked Jay. "Dexter's probably out on the greenhouse porch. He wants to buy some plants. Where were you, anyway?"

"Hurry now, talk later," said Cindy. "I'll explain everything when we find Dexter."

They walked through the other rooms to the glassed-in porch. They saw Alex Baxter just ahead.

Dexter was setting some small cactus plants aside. He looked up when Jay and Cindy entered. "Hey, these are great cactus plants," he said. "I'm going to buy six."

Alex Baxter glanced at the boys. He and the members of the Spotlight Club were alone on the greenhouse porch. He shut the door.

Dexter looked at Alex Baxter, then at Cindy and the closed door. "What's going on?" he asked, pushing his glasses up.

"This is Alex Baxter," said Cindy quickly. "This is Dexter Tate, and this is my brother, Jay Temple." Alex Baxter shook their hands.

"Alex Baxter is a detective," said Cindy.

The boys stared. Jay's eyebrows went up.

Alex Baxter reached into his wallet and withdrew a card. He handed it to Dexter. Jay and Cindy looked over Dexter's shoulder as he read out loud:

ALEX BAXTER

DETECTIVE INVESTIGATOR

CBI, LTD.

CHICAGO BRANCH

There was a Chicago address and telephone number under that.

Dexter whistled. "Gee, we didn't know you were a detective!"

"Of course you didn't," said Alex Baxter. "Naturally I couldn't tell anyone. And I never would have told you, even now, if it hadn't been for this young lady. She had started to suspect me—and no wonder. A series of happenings, an unfortunate series of events, forced me into the open, as it were. But only with you," he said earnestly. "If these crook suspect that I am a detective, they will run away before we have a chance to arrest them. And we must arrest them."

Cindy's head was spinning. "These crooks? What crooks?"

Alex Baxter glanced through the window set in the porch door. "Come over here," he whispered. "No one must see that we are talking together." He led the way to a far corner.

"I have to confide in you. I can't have you calling Tom Foster's attention to me. Then he would know they'd been found. They would disappear again."

Cindy started to ask a question. It was all confusing. Alex Baxter stopped her. "Don't talk. There isn't time. I'll tell you everything tomorrow. But now we must move quickly. We must find it before Jenny Mayflower returns."

Find it? Find what? wondered Cindy. He must mean the iron dog. They'd have to tell him they had it. And what about Jenny Mayflower?

"Let me explain," Alex Baxter continued. "Jenny Mayflower and Tom Foster are a very clever pair of crooks. Very clever indeed. We've been on to them for a long time. They are what we call in the trade 'con artists.' That means they play a confidence game."

"What's that—a confidence game?" asked Dexter.

"They appear to be a nice, simple, honest, likeable couple. They get people to have confidence in them. That way they are able to trick people into believing anything. Anything and everything!"

"Believing what?" asked Jay.

"Like this," explained Alex Baxter quickly. "Jenny Mayflower has been Mrs. Melanie Wellington's secretary and companion for several months.

She's gained her confidence and love. Now she's ready to rob Mrs. Wellington of her possessions, her very home! And Tom Foster works with her. This isn't the first time they've tricked an old, mixed-up lady." His voice broke. He seemed to be very angry.

"Jenny—" thought Cindy aloud. "No wonder Mrs. Wellington trusted her. Who wouldn't?"

"I don't get it," said Jay. "What did she steal anyway?"

Cindy thought quickly. What did she steal, after all? Was all this fuss about an iron dog? And what did he mean about stealing Mrs. Wellington's house?

Alex Baxter seemed not to hear Jay's question. "Let me continue," he said. "We haven't much time. I can fill you in later on all the details." He rubbed his chin. "This couple has pulled the same trick many times before, but we have never been able to prove anything. We have never been able to make an arrest, an arrest that will stick. Now we are very close, but we need this final proof. Otherwise they will slip through our fingers one more time." He looked at each of the Spotlighters in turn. "You must help me, you *must*."

"How can we help you?" asked Jay.

Cindy's heart pounded. Jenny and Tom crooks? It just couldn't be true.

Alex Baxter glanced at Cindy. "Jenny Mayflower has told you that she is to marry this Tom Foster."

"In three days," whispered Cindy.

Alex Baxter shook his head. "That's one more of their lies," he said. "Actually we believe them to be brother and sister."

"I don't understand," Cindy said, weakly.

"This is how they work," Alex Baxter said, leaning forward. "Jenny Mayflower takes a job with a nice rich old lady, like Mrs. Wellington. A nice rich lady with a big house. She gains the old lady's confidence. Next she introduces Tom. They get the old lady to move into an old people's home. For her own good, they say. They talk her into letting them handle selling her house and everything in it. The old lady never suspects a thing."

The Spotlight Clubbers stared.

"You know what happens next? It's happening right here! Jenny Mayflower and Tom Foster—those are just names they are using this time—have sold this house. Now they're selling everything in it. For cash. They have the money from the house and from the sale and they disappear. They move fast. Nobody has any time to ask questions. The sale of the household goods is just announced the day before it begins. They're clever! We've got to catch them before it is too late."

"So Jenny and Tom will leave today?" asked Dexter. Alex Baxter nodded. "Exactly. You'll see. No one from Kenoska will ever hear from them again. They will move to another town, use other names.

They will find another old lady. Unless we stop them. Unless we stop them—you and I."

Cindy's thoughts were racing. "But that's not true, what you said about Jenny and Tom. It can't be! It just can't!"

Alex Baxter shrugged his shoulders. "Young lady, this is going to be very hard for you. Perhaps you should not try to be a detective. It is a very sad, very difficult business. To accuse someone you like…" He turned to Jay. "It is difficult for your sister. I am so sorry."

Cindy squared her shoulders. "Jenny told me she was going to spend the whole day at her new apartment. She has to wait there for the furniture to be moved in. And then Tom is going to meet her there. And then they're going to drive to the airport to meet Tom's parents." Cindy looked down at the floor. "She was so excited."

Alex Baxter stared at her. "Do you still believe that?" he asked gently.

Cindy nodded. Then she shook her head miserably. "I don't know what I believe."

"Everyone trusts Jenny," Alex Baxter said with a smile. "Everyone. You are not alone."

A Detective!

Cindy looked at Alex Baxter. He understood how she felt. He didn't seem to want anything for himself.

Jay nudged her. "See? Just because you like people doesn't mean they can't be bad guys. If you're a detective you have to suspect people you like as much as you suspect people you don't like."

Alex Baxter flashed his narrow teeth at Jay. "I can see you're a fine detective already, young man."

Jay flushed.

"And now," Alex Baxter said, lowering his voice and looking over their heads, "I see Tom Foster looking in our direction for the second time. It won't do to arouse his suspicions. Agreed?" He looked at the three detectives. They nodded slowly.

Dropping his voice still more, he said, "We must leave. All of us. We cannot have Tom Foster link us together. You three leave first. Go to one of your homes. Which shall it be?"

The Spotlighters looked at each other. What else could they do but obey? Cindy thought of the iron dog under her bed. They should go there. "Our house," she said. "It's the white one with the big porch."

She glanced at Jay and Dexter. All three were thinking one thing. She should tell Alex Baxter about the iron dog. But Cindy held back. She had to talk with Jay and Dexter first. Anyway Alex Baxter was giving directions.

"All three of you must watch this house very closely. You must make sure that Tom does not leave without your seeing him."

"He's not leaving until three thirty," said Cindy. "That's what he and Jenny said, anyway."

Alex Baxter turned to her. His eyes narrowed until they became slits. "Young lady, I have told you once, twice, three times. You cannot trust either of them."

He patted his pockets and frowned. "I'll need your telephone number. And both of your addresses." He patted another pocket. "Ah, here we are." He drew out a small black notebook and flipped the pages with his long fingers.

He's got a notebook too, thought Cindy.

"And now—your telephone numbers, your addresses."

Alex Baxter touched his pencil to his teeth. He wrote down everything.

A Detective!

"What shall we do when we see Tom leave the house?" asked Jay. "How can we follow him if he has a car?"

"It will not be necessary to follow him," Alex Baxter said. "One of the other detectives assigned to this case is out on the street now, waiting in a car parked behind Tom's car. The way I waited behind Jenny Mayflower's car. As soon as Tom leaves, my partner will follow. And Tom will lead us to Jenny. They both will be behind bars tonight!" He smiled at them.

Cindy's heart was pounding. Jenny and Tom in jail! She could hardly believe it.

Dexter pushed his glasses up on his nose. "But why should we watch if someone is waiting behind Tom's car?"

Alex Baxter smiled a patient smile. "Because he may not take his car. He may go on foot. Now my telephone number is on my card. I want you to telephone that number the moment you see Tom leaving."

"It's a Chicago number," said Dexter. "And it will take you an hour to drive to Chicago."

"I have an answering service," Alex Baxter said quickly. "Just leave your message. I call in every half hour and get any messages left for me. I keep track of other detectives on the case too. I will call you about developments and instructions."

Cindy tried to think. Should they tell him they had the iron dog? It must be an important piece of evidence.

"You were looking for something when you came in," said Cindy. "You thought it was in that package. But it was just an old vase."

"You are a very observant young lady," smiled Alex Baxter. "Indeed I was looking for something.

"Something very, very important to this case. I was looking for a doorstop—a doorstop in the shape of a dog. Without it, we cannot prove our case against Jenny Mayflower and Tom Foster."

Cindy's head was spinning. "Why can't you prove your case? Why is a doorstop important?" she asked.

They would have to tell him! They would have to. Still she held back. Now wasn't the time.

Alex Baxter strode to the glass door and looked out. "We must move quickly," he said. "Tom Foster has looked in this direction again."

A Detective!

"What if Jenny comes back?" asked Dexter. "Should we call you then?"

"She won't be coming back," said Alex Baxter positively. "She and Tom are going to meet outside of town. We'll pick them up at that point, if all goes well." He glanced at them and smiled. "It's really been a piece of luck for me to run across such fine, clever detectives. You go now. Act as if nothing has happened. I'll leave in a few minutes." He walked out the door and through the dining room.

The three detectives stared after him. And then they stared at each other.

"We have to tell him that we have the iron dog," whispered Dexter. "He says it's the real proof. The real proof that Tom Foster and Jenny Mayflower are crooks!"

"We're concealing evidence," Jay said.

"Let's tell him when we call on the telephone," suggested Cindy. "We have to talk first. We have to *prove* what we know—that Tom Foster hid the iron dog in the snowman."

Dexter groaned. "Mr. Hooley's Rule coming up!"

"Right," said Cindy. "We can't tell a real detective a thing we haven't proved ourselves."

"But we can prove that we have the dog," said Jay.

"But that's *all* we can prove," answered Cindy. "Let's go over our notes and then call him."

"I'll settle for anything," agreed Dexter. "As long as we get something to eat. I'm starved." He walked over to pick up the cactus plants he had set aside. "Can't forget these!"

The Spotlighters walked to the front door. Many people were coming and going. Someone was paying Tom for a silver teapot. He was smiling and wrapping it in tissue paper.

Dexter paid for his cactus plants. "Better watch these," grinned Tom. "They bite. Anyway, they prickle."

They said good-bye. "See you later," called Tom as they were leaving. "My parents are coming tonight. They love kids and they never see any. They'll be here all day tomorrow. Why don't you come on over? Dad would love to tell you all he knows about cactus plants."

"Sure," said Dexter.

They walked in the snow to the Temples' house.

A Detective!

As soon as the door had closed behind them, Dexter gave a war whoop.

"What's that about?" asked Cindy.

"I'm so tired of whispering," he shouted. "It's great to talk out loud again."

"I hear you're back," called Mrs. Temple from upstairs. "And I'd bet my whole free day that you have another mystery!"

"You're right, Mom," called Cindy.

"We've got a billion things to talk about," Jay told Dexter and Cindy. "You two watch the red house and I'll fix some sandwiches. I'm dying of starvation."

"Good," said Cindy. "I'd rather watch than fix."

In a moment Cindy and Dexter saw Alex Baxter leave the Wellington house, his long black coat and wide black hat etched against the white snow.

She and Dexter watched him stride to the end of the street and walk around the barricade. Then he climbed into the green car with the crumpled fender. In a moment he was gone.

"It's funny," said Cindy. "I was so sure he was a bad guy. And all along he was a detective trying to prove that Jenny and Tom were the guilty ones." She stared outside. "I still don't believe it," she decided. "I believe it with my head, but I don't believe it in my bones."

Dexter sighed. "Your bones!"

Jay came in with a platter of sandwich fixings.

"And mugs of soup!" said Cindy. "Thank you, Jay!"

In a few minutes they had finished lunch. Many people were going in and out of the red house. People were coming out with their arms filled with packages.

"The sale seems to be doing all right," said Jay. "They must be making money."

"We have to watch sharp to see if one of those people leaving the house is Tom. He could be disguised," said Dexter.

"He couldn't be disguised as a very little, very old lady," said Jay.

They were still watching when Mrs. Temple left with the Tates for Chicago.

CHAPTER 7
The Warning Fails

CINDY WAS LEAFING through her notebook for the tenth time. "It's funny," she said, "that Alex Baxter is letting Jenny and Tom sell Mrs. Wellington's things. He knows they're guilty. Why doesn't he stop them now?"

"Because a detective has to have proof," said Jay. "That's what he was telling us."

"And the iron dog is proof," said Dexter, pushing his glasses up on his head.

"Right. And we have the iron dog," said Jay.

"But he doesn't know we have it," said Dexter. "Nobody knows but us."

"And nobody should know," said Cindy. "We have

to be able to prove how it got into the snowman before we let Alex Baxter know we have it. Otherwise, we're not helping at all."

Suddenly Jay clapped a hand to his head.

"You've thought of something!" said Dexter.

"I've thought of my paper route," answered Jay. "Just as things start happening, I'll be off on my paper route! Delivering papers when I should be solving mysteries."

"Call Travis Hackworthy," suggested Dexter. "Ask him if he'll sub for you."

So Jay called Travis and arranged for him to deliver the afternoon papers for his route.

Cindy was writing in her notebook. "If we can prove once and for all that Tom Foster stole the iron dog and hid it in the snowman, we can really help Alex Baxter. Here's what we know so far: Tom Foster helped the Maxwell kids with the snowman. We know that because of the sunglasses and the scarf. He sent Amy and Randy into the house for a carrot. That's when he could have hidden the iron dog."

"Could have, could have," said Jay. "We have to have real proof before we call Alex Baxter."

The Warning Fails

"I wish he had told us why that iron dog is so important," said Dexter. "But he was in such a hurry."

Cindy chewed her pencil. "I still can't believe Jenny's a crook."

"Here we go again," groaned Jay.

"Cindy, remember the time you really liked that usher character in a movie?" asked Dexter. "You were so sure he couldn't have been the crook because he had such a nice smile. And because he was polite."

"Well, he was polite," said Cindy.

"Sure, but it turned out he was a crook," Dexter said. "I think we ought to have a new rule. The Usher Rule. The rule that says you have to try just as hard to prove someone you like is guilty as you try to prove someone you don't like is guilty. See how long it took me to say that? And now all we have to say is the Usher Rule."

"OK," agreed Cindy. "And you're right. The reason that Tom and Jenny are so good at this confidence racket is because they seem so nice."

"The Usher Rule," Jay said to himself. "Good."

Cindy turned another page in her notebook.

"Oh, here's something I forgot to tell you. When I went upstairs in Mrs. Wellington's house there was a long hall. That's when I scared myself stiff seeing my reflection in the big mirror at the end of the hall. Anyway, there were lots of different doors that opened into the hall, only they were all closed. That's what made it so dark. All but one, and that was strange too. The door was open and I saw flowers in the room. Why? I thought the house was empty."

"It doesn't make sense," Jay said thoughtfully.

"Nothing makes sense," said Dexter.

"But everything will, once we talk to Alex Baxter again," said Cindy. "This time we'll have time to ask him questions."

Cindy copied her notes. The boys kept watch. Dozens of people had come to the sale, come and gone. But not Tom Foster.

"Maybe he sneaked out the back door," said Jay.

"We'd have seen him," said Dexter.

It was beginning to grow dark. "We won't be able to see him if he doesn't leave pretty soon," complained Dexter.

The Warning Fails

Just as he spoke, Jay grabbed Dexter's arm. "There he is!" he whispered.

Sure enough, Tom Foster was just coming out of the front door of the red house. He had the metal box under his arm. Filled with money, thought Cindy. Tom started to walk down the street toward the construction barricade.

"Remember, one of the detectives is waiting in the car behind Tom's," whispered Dexter. "He'll follow him."

"We've got to call Alex Baxter," said Jay, reaching for the telephone.

"Wait until Tom gets to the barricade. And opens his car," suggested Cindy.

"We can't see that far. It's too dark," said Dexter.

Jay picked up the telephone. He looked at the card Alex Baxter had given them.

In a moment a woman's voice answered, "May I help you?"

"I want to leave a message for Alex Baxter," said Jay.

"Your name, please?"

"Jay Temple," said Jay. "Tell him Tom Foster has

left the house. And wait a minute," continued Jay, looking at Dexter and then at Cindy. "Tell him we have the dog he was looking for."

"Very well," said the voice. "Thank you."

Jay stood holding the telephone a minute. Then he hung up. "That's all," he said. "The end of the mystery."

"Not quite," said Cindy. "When he comes to get the dog we can ask him why it's so important to the case. Why he needs it to prove that Jenny and Tom are guilty."

The Spotlighters looked through the deepening dark to the red house. "What will Mrs. Wellington think when Jenny and Tom don't come to see her tonight?" asked Cindy. "She'll be waiting for them to come with Tom's parents. And they'll never come. Because there aren't any parents and there isn't any wedding. Jenny and Tom are running off with the money from the sale and the house."

Suddenly Cindy jumped up. "We have to tell Mrs. Wellington! We can't let her sit there and wait and wait. And then hear all about it from strangers—policemen and detectives—tomorrow. Let's find her and tell her tonight. There's nothing more we can do here, anyway."

The Warning Fails

"How can we find her?" asked Dexter.

Cindy picked up her notebook and started flipping through the pages. "Here it is. The North Star. Jenny says Mrs. Wellington lives there now. Let's look it up."

"It's out on Cypress Drive," said Jay in a moment, "on the other side of town."

"We can take a bus," said Dexter. "It's a long ride, but we can get there."

"Good," said Cindy. "I like it when we're doing something about something. I'm tired of just sitting and thinking."

Soon the three detectives were running to the bus stop. In a few minutes the bus pulled up to the curb.

"What if Mrs. Wellington won't see us?" asked Cindy. "You remember what Alex Baxter said about her—she's old and feeble. She doesn't really know what's going on."

"I still don't know why Mr. Baxter hasn't told her anything about Jenny and Tom," added Jay. "It's only fair she should know. It's her house after all."

"Maybe he was afraid she'd tell Jenny," said Dexter. "And then Jenny would run off with her brother Tom."

They left the bus at the Franklin Street stop. Cypress Street was just a short walk beyond the bus stop.

"Well, here we are," Cindy said, staring across the snow-covered lawn. A long building lay before them, with lights shining in almost every window.

They started up the long walk to the front door. As they walked into the building, a woman seated at a desk glanced at them.

Cindy spoke up. "We'd like to visit Mrs. Melanie Wellington, if we may." The three detectives looked at the lady behind the desk.

"Oh, how lovely," the lady said. "Mrs. Wellington is in Apartment 14." She turned halfway around in her chair. "You follow this first corridor and then turn left by the double doors, and there you are!"

The Spotlighters thanked her and walked where she had directed. They passed a large room with many tables in it. Some people were playing cards and laughing. Others were sitting, talking quietly.

"I thought it was an old people's home," said Cindy. "These people don't look old at all!"

They found Apartment 14 and hesitated just

The Warning Fails

outside the door. "Remember," Cindy whispered. "We'll tell her about Jenny first." The boys nodded. Cindy knocked softly on the door three times.

"I'll be right there!" called a voice from inside. The door opened and they faced a tall, elegant lady. Thin lines of gray hair swirled into brown curls on top of her head. She was dressed in a beautiful long gown. Sparkling earrings hung in small loops from her ears. Her big brown eyes looked down at the children in a friendly way.

"Mrs. Wellington?" asked Cindy, hesitating.

The woman smiled and nodded. "And to what do I owe this honor?" she asked, her eyes twinkling. "Come in, come in." She stretched a slender arm toward her living room.

The Spotlighters looked at each other. Cindy thought, Why she's not a little old lady at all. She's beautiful.

This time it was Dexter who spoke first. "Mrs. Wellington, I'm Dexter Tate, and these are my friends, Jay and Cindy Temple. We've come to warn you." He stopped and looked at Jay and Cindy.

"Warn me? Warn me about what?" asked Mrs. Wellington. "I daresay this is a most interesting evening. Do tell me what you're about."

Cindy cleared her throat and then spoke in a rush. "Mrs. Wellington, it's about Jenny Mayflower. She's been lying to you all this time. She's sold your house and she's going to run away with Tom Foster and all the money. They had a house sale today and sold all your nice things. And they're not really getting married at all. They're brother and sister."

Mrs. Wellington stared at the children for a moment. Then she burst out laughing, "Oh dear, oh dear."

"It's true," insisted Dexter. "You'll never see Jenny Mayflower again."

Mrs. Wellington leaned against a chair and then collapsed into it, laughing. Finally she wiped her eyes with her long trailing silk scarf. "I'm afraid you'd better start from the beginning," she said.

Cindy looked helplessly at Dexter and Jay.

"Oh, but you must all sit down," Mrs. Wellington said. "Let me pull some chairs up." She was standing before the three detectives had a chance to move.

The Warning Fails

"From the beginning," said Mrs. Wellington, when they were all sitting down.

Cindy opencd her mouth to speak, but Mrs. Wellington jumped up from her chair again. "With all this going on, I forgot I was the hostess. Would you like some hot chocolate? I can fix some in a jiffy."

Without waiting for an answer, she flew across the room and went through a swinging door.

"Poor lady," Cindy sighed. "It's going to be sad when she hears the truth. And she's going to be hard to convince."

Jay, Dexter, and Cindy looked around them. There were paintings in frames on the walls. Dexter got up from his chair to look at one of the paintings. "Hey," he said, "the signature on this says Melanie Wellington."

"And here's a portrait of Jenny," said Cindy. "That makes me feel even worse about telling her."

A moment later Mrs. Wellington appeared with a silver tray, laden with cups and saucers.

"We were looking at your paintings," Cindy said. "You're an artist!"

"Painting is a new hobby with me," Mrs. Wellington

said. "In that big old house would you believe I could never find a room to paint? I really love it here!"

Cindy saw something else framed and hanging on the wall. "Is this a poem?" she asked.

"Oh, it's a sampler," Mrs. Wellington explained. "It's a riddle my husband and I made up when we moved into the old red house."

Cindy read the riddle silently. "I can't guess it," she said. "Do you mind if I copy it?"

Mrs. Wellington passed the boys their chocolate and gave Cindy a cup when she sat down. "Once again—begin at the beginning," she said.

"Well," Cindy started, "Jenny Mayflower isn't at all what you think. She's selling all your things and your house and she's going to keep all the money. She and Tom Foster are going to run away with it."

Mrs. Wellington smiled at Cindy. "But dear, they're doing no such thing. Jenny is the kindest, dearest girl I've known. She and Tom are getting married this week. A wonderful young man, that Tom."

"But they wouldn't even let you come back to your own house!" exclaimed Dexter. "They made you sign papers to sell it. And they're not even going to give you the money for it."

"I think someone has absolutely been pulling your legs," laughed Mrs. Wellington.

"But then why are you here instead of in your own house?" asked Cindy. "You can't even go back now because they sold your house."

Mrs. Wellington shook her head. "I don't *want* to live in that big old house. I love it here. Can't you see?" She spread her arms and looked around her apartment. "Everything that I could possibly want is here. There are so many people here my own age. We play cards. We even gamble! And it's so cheerful, having someone to talk to about old times. It was my decision to move here. Nobody else's."

Cindy sat up straighter. "But, Mrs. Wellington, what about all those things in your house that Jenny and Tom sold? What about the money they took?"

Mrs. Wellington leaned over the table and picked up a cookie. "I can see it's time I got some answers from you. What on earth makes you think all these strange things have happened?"

Jay looked from Dexter to Cindy. He cleared his throat. "A detective told us," he said quietly. "He's known about Jenny Mayflower and Tom Foster for a long time. It's true, Mrs. Wellington. They *are* crooks. They go from one town to another, finding rich old ladies to cheat."

Cindy poked him.

"I mean rich ladies," said Dexter.

"Anyway," interrupted Jay, "they're con artists. Playing a confidence game. They're selling your house. They're having a neighborhood sale just so they can get as much cash as they can in the shortest time. They've already stolen and sold all the valuable things."

"Yes," Cindy said. "And Mr. Baxter, the detective, told us—"

Melanie Wellington held up a jeweled hand. "Mr. Baxter? Mr. Alex Baxter?"

"Why, yes," said Cindy in surprise.

"But, my darlings," she smiled, "Alex Baxter is my nephew! My terrible, talented nephew!"

CHAPTER 8
Secret of the Iron Dog

THE THREE DETECTIVES stared at Melanie Wellington and then at each other.

"Your nephew?" asked Cindy.

"Oh, yes, my sweethearts, my nephew. He's no more a detective than the man in the moon. He doesn't have time to be a detective. He's a full-time, all-time liar." And Mrs. Wellington exploded into laughter.

She wiped her eyes with her long flowing scarf. "Forgive me, my darlings," she said. "This is too delicious, too delicious. Alex Baxter, detective! What next?" She leaned forward and beckoned them closer. "He's a fraud, my beautifuls, a *born* fraud. I don't blame you for being taken in by his cunning. He's fooled me too. Many times."

She leaned back and took another sip of hot chocolate. "He comes over occasionally. Usually to get something out of me. I wondered why he came over yesterday. A most unwelcome visit, I can assure you. He absolutely stormed in, all black, all fire. A black coat, black hat, black gloves, black boots, black hair, black eyebrows, black eyes, and a black look."

She paused and tilted her head back, her eyes half closed, smiling. "I have a confession to make. I don't like him—my own nephew! I never have. He's really quite terrible. A greedy, clever man. And now he's been telling you some very naughty tales. Pay no attention."

"But, Mrs. Wellington," Cindy said finally, "he gave us his card. It was printed and everything. It says, 'Alex Baxter, Detective Investigator.' And there's a Chicago address and telephone number. I've got it with me, I'll show you."

Mrs. Wellington held up her hand. "No need to show me, dear one. I trust he's made lots of cards like that. All with a different profession under his name."

"But he told us about the other detectives who work with him," said Jay. "And he has an answering service."

"He can't be lying," protested Dexter, frowning.

"And why not?" asked Mrs. Wellington. "He's playing this nasty joke on you because he's greedy and wants something. I'll tell you why he came to see me. He was looking for an iron doorstop. It's in the shape of a dog and very charming. He knows its secret, but he doesn't know the *whole* secret. He just knows it's valuable. I know the whole secret. Nobody else knows a thing about it."

The Spotlighters looked at each other. Mrs. Wellington went on. "I knew at once he was looking for it. I'm not quite sure how he figured it out, but he wanted that dog. He's a clever young man, you know. A pity he didn't turn all his genius to something good. Ah, well," she sighed. "But to go on. He stormed in like a thunder cloud. I looked at him and said, 'Now, now, Alex.' He was all sweetness then. 'Aunt Melanie this,' 'Aunt Melanie that.' A very convincing act, but he didn't fool me. He looked in every nook and cranny. And then I said, 'Alex Baxter, spit it out. You're looking for that dog.' He looked at me with big innocent eyes and shook his head. 'But you're not going to get it,' I told him. 'Jenny has the dog and is bringing it over to me.' He scowled at me then. You know his scowl."

She paused and sipped from her cup. "And then I told him my plan," she continued. "That I have a special surprise for Jenny and Tom. And that it has to do with the doorstop." Her eyes twinkled at the three detectives. "And they have no idea! I love surprises. Tonight we're going to have a wonderful party at my old house. They're going to pick me up here. Tom's parents will be there too. And then the surprise!" She smiled at them over her cup. "When I told Alex about my plan, he was so angry he could barely speak. I told him he was altogether too greedy and wanted everything for nothing. But this is the one thing he won't get his hands on."

The Spotlighters looked at each other. Cindy asked softly, "What if Alex Baxter got the iron dog?"

Mrs. Wellington sat up straight. "Oh, it would be terrible, just terrible!" She stared at Cindy. "He doesn't have it, does he?"

Cindy quickly leaned forward. "We have it, Mrs. Wellington. We have the iron dog."

"Oh, that's beautiful," sighed Mrs. Wellington.

"You have the dog. And Alex is probably looking *everywhere* for it." She suddenly turned toward Cindy. "You haven't told him you have it, have you?"

"Yes," Cindy said weakly. "We left a message for him with his answering service this afternoon."

Mrs. Wellington gasped. "You told him you have the dog?"

Cindy twisted her hands. "He was so convincing. We were sure we were doing the right thing."

Mrs. Wellington frowned and tapped her foot. "Just like him to twist your mind in his direction. This is not good, not good at all." She looked at the detectives. "Does he know where you live?"

Cindy nodded.

"Then you must leave this instant." She stood up, her scarf trailing behind her. "Get home as quickly as you can. You must make sure that the dog is safe. You must not let Alex have it!"

She rushed to the door of her apartment and opened it. "Hurry, dears. There's no time to lose. You must keep the dog safe. Bring it to the red house when you see all the lights turned on. Can you do it?" she asked, staring down at them.

"Of course we can," said Jay. "You'll see."

The Spotlighters filed quickly through the door.

"And do be careful!" called Mrs. Wellington after them. "I can't tell you how important this is."

"Wow!" Dexter breathed when they were outside the building. "How many times can we be wrong in one day?"

The air was colder now. They hurried to the bus stop.

"I wish we were home now," Cindy said. "What is it about that dog? I've looked at it and looked at it, but I can't figure it out."

"It must be filled with money," said Jay. "I'll bet it is."

"It must be," Dexter said. "No wonder he wants it so much."

Cindy stared out the bus window and shivered. "I wonder where Alex Baxter is now. What if he's waiting right outside our house?"

The three detectives were silent for a minute.

"Why do only Mrs. Wellington and Alex Baxter know what's so important about the dog?" asked Jay. "Why not Jenny?"

"I guess Mrs. Wellington wanted it to be a secret from Jenny so she could surprise her," Cindy said. "But how did Alex Baxter find out about it?"

The bus stopped and the three detectives got off. Shadows moved in and out among the houses and trees. Was one of the shadows Alex Baxter's?

"Let's make a run for it to our house," whispered Jay. They darted across the street.

"I'll grab the key," Jay said, hurrying ahead of Dexter and Cindy. "Mom always leaves it in the same place."

They let themselves in the front door.

"The dog's in my room," called Cindy, as she dashed up the stairs, two steps at a time. The boys raced up

after her. She pulled down the window shade and turned on her light. She took the dog out from under her bed. She'd half expected it to be gone.

They sat in a circle on the floor, staring at the iron doorstop. Dexter picked it up. "Maybe it has something to do with the iron ball in its mouth," he said, putting his fingers around the ball. He tried to twist it and turn it, but it didn't budge.

"There just has to be money in there," said Jay, frowning. "It must open. Let me try it." He took the dog from Dexter and turned it upside down. He tapped it. "It's empty," he reported. "Hollow." He shook it hard for a minute, holding it close to his ear.

Cindy took the iron doorstop from Jay. She stared at the collar around its neck. Then she ran her fingers along it. "There's something…" She grasped the head firmly and suddenly there was a slight grating noise. She twisted the head slowly around and unscrewed it from the body.

"It's empty!" breathed Dexter, peering into the iron dog. "I don't believe it. Who could have taken the money out?"

"There's got to be something inside here," said Jay, taking the dog and shaking it. Nothing fell out.

Cindy was peering into the head. "I can't see anything," she said, frowning. She poked her fingers up into the head. "But I can *feel* something in here!"

"What is it?" asked Jay, leaning toward Cindy.

"I can't tell," Cindy said. "It's something hard and small, but it's stuck to something. It's stuck to wax."

She pushed her fingers into the head again. "I'm getting it loose," she said excitedly. Dexter and Jay leaned closer. A minute later Cindy cried out, "I've got it!"

She drew her hand out, and the three detectives stared at the small object in Cindy's palm.

Dexter whistled. "A key!"

Cindy scraped the rest of the wax off the key and held it up. "So this is what Alex Baxter wanted!"

"It wasn't the doorstop after all. It was the key all the time. But what good is a key without a keyhole?" asked Dexter.

Cindy stared at the key in her hand. "Wait a minute," she said slowly. "I just heard or read something about a key. I'm sure I did."

"What was it?" asked Jay.

"I can't remember," Cindy said.

"That helps," commented Dexter.

"Let me look in my notebook," Cindy said, reaching into her coat pocket.

"Always her notebook!" sighed Jay. "You'd think she couldn't eat unless she checked her notebook first."

"You're always glad I have it and that I write everything down," said Cindy. "I just *know* I saw something about a key somewhere." She turned the pages, frowning at each one.

"Here! I knew I was right. Look." She showed the boys what she had written.

"I don't get it," Jay said. "What is it?"

"Remember when I asked Mrs. Wellington what the poem in the sampler meant?" Cindy asked.

The boys nodded.

"She said it was a riddle. I wrote it down so that later I could figure it out by myself. Look at the title."

"The Secret Key," read Jay. "You were right about a key," he said to Cindy.

Cindy frowned and tapped her pencil on her notebook. "Listen while I read it. See if you can think of anything it could mean.

> I meet someone beneath the owl—
> That someone seems to me to scowl.
> I smile and see that someone smile,
> We stay together all the while."

"What's that business about an owl?" asked Dexter. "Where would you ever meet an owl? Except in a woods somewhere."

"I don't get it," said Jay. "And who's staying together all the while? Does that mean forever?"

"I think so," Cindy said. "But the owl...the owl." She leaned against her bed and stared up at the ceiling.

Suddenly her eyes widened and she sat up straight. "Could it be?" she muttered. "Of course it is! The mirror upstairs on the door! It's at the end of the hall. I remember there's an owl etched at the top. And the rest of the riddle fits too. When I was walking down that hallway, it was dark. I thought it was Jenny coming toward me, but it was my reflection. No matter what I do in front of the mirror, my reflection does the same thing. And that's what the riddle means!"

Dexter and Jay stared at Cindy. Jay said, "So the key must unlock something behind the mirror!"

"Alex Baxter was there, in Mrs. Wellington's apartment this morning," said Dexter, excitedly. "He must know the sampler. Maybe he's figured it out!"

"We have to go over there," Jay said. "We have to unlock whatever this key unlocks before Alex Baxter gets there."

"We have to keep whatever it is safe until Jenny and Tom come back with Tom's parents and Mrs. Wellington," Cindy said.

"Let's go!" said Jay. He grabbed a flashlight.

Cindy shoved the two parts of the dog back under her bed and put the key in her pocket.

CHAPTER 9
Who Can Be Trusted?

MOMENTS LATER THE Spotlighters stood in front of the red house. They stared up at the dark windows. They huddled together. It was no use to try the front door. It was sure to be locked.

"What if Alex Baxter is inside?" asked Dexter.

Cindy looked around and murmured, "Let's not think about it. Let's just get in ourselves."

They walked around the side of the house. The windows were too high to reach.

"I've got it!" whispered Dexter. "The greenhouse windows! I remember one window was open a little. There was a note attached to one of the cactus plants about watching for the draft."

Jay and Cindy followed Dexter as he ran to the greenhouse. It took them a moment to find the right window. Jay hissed, "Here's the one. It's open just a crack, but it pulls out." He lifted the window out toward him. "I'll crawl in first. Then Cindy can follow me, and then Dexter."

"Oh, let's hurry," said Cindy. "Quietly."

Dexter and Cindy stood in the snow, their teeth chattering. Jay was halfway through the window when they heard a muffled cry.

"What is it?" whispered Dexter, leaning toward the window.

Jay's voice whispered back, "A cactus plant. Once I get through I'll push them aside so you won't land on top of them."

He helped pull Cindy into the greenhouse. Then Dexter followed, and they were finally standing inside.

"We've got to hurry," said Jay. "Cindy, you've got the key?"

Cindy patted her pocket. "Right here."

"Then let's find the lock," Dexter said. "Cindy, you lead the way. You know where the mirror is."

Cindy made her way through the greenhouse and found the door to the dining room. "This way," she whispered. They stood in the dark dining room and listened.

"I don't hear anything," Cindy whispered. She walked over to the door leading to the kitchen, and the boys followed. They all stood for a moment in the kitchen. Then Cindy said, "This way," and led them to the back stairway she had found earlier. "The steps are pretty steep," she whispered over her shoulder.

The boys followed her as she started up the stairs.

"How can you see where you're going?" asked Jay in a whisper, close behind Cindy.

"I can't," she answered. "But I've been here before, and I remember." A step creaked beneath her.

"We're almost at the top," she breathed. Was Alex Baxter standing up there in the hall, waiting?

The three detectives reached the top of the stairs and stopped. They tried to stare down the long hall toward the mirrored door.

Who Can Be Trusted?

They listened. Not a sound. The hallway had an empty feel, but they could be wrong. "It's too dark to see anything," muttered Jay. He clicked on his flashlight, and the Spotlighters faced a bright circle of light, reflected from the mirror.

They walked toward the mirror. "That's it," whispered Cindy, pointing. "That's the owl."

The boys nodded and stared up at the owl.

Cindy touched the little key in her pocket. Then she stooped to hunt for the keyhole beneath the doorknob.

"No!" she exclaimed softly. "The key for this door is right here in the lock. It's a big key, not like the one from the iron dog."

"Turn it anyway and let's see what's behind the door," Jay said.

Cindy turned the key in the lock and Jay turned the doorknob. The door opened easily—and it led into a deep, stuffy closet!

"It has to be a *little* keyhole," Cindy whispered.

"But where?" asked Dexter.

"We'll just have to look," said Cindy. "And hope Alex Baxter wasn't here first."

The Spotlighters studied the mirror as closely as they could in the shadows. They ran their fingers around the edge. Not a clue!

"Maybe the keyhole is inside," said Dexter. "In the closet. There's a lot of stuff. It's going to take time to search every corner."

Things were piled neatly in boxes on shelves. If Alex Baxter had been here, he would surely have pulled things apart.

"This calls for speed," Jay said, flashing his light into the corners of the closet.

Cindy's heart sank. Nothing looked even a little like a keyhole. She thought about the riddle. "I think we're wrong," she said. "The keyhole has to have something to do with the mirror to fit the riddle."

Again they studied the door of the closet. "Where would a keyhole be?" murmured Cindy. She ran her fingers along the narrow edge of the door.

Cindy pushed the door catch back and let it spring out. Then she felt the hardware under the catch. She felt something small—maybe where a screw might be missing.

Who Can Be Trusted?

"Here! Shine the flashlight here," she begged Jay. And where no one would be expected to notice, Cindy found a tiny keyhole.

Fingers shaking, Cindy took the key out of her pocket. She closed her eyes for a second and crossed the fingers of her left hand.

"Here goes," she said, pushing the key into the lock. She turned it and there was a click.

Suddenly the mirror on the door swung out as if a spring had been released. It just missed the boys. The three detectives stared. A shallow storage place had been chiseled out of the wood of the door behind the mirror.

Wedged in that small space was a flat leather case.

"Wow!" breathed Dexter. "A secret storage space!"

"Let's see what's here," Jay whispered and lifted out the case. He set it gently on the floor and stared up at Dexter and Cindy.

"Ready?" he asked.

Dexter and Cindy crouched down on the floor next to him. "Ready," they said together.

Jay unclasped the case and opened the lid. They all peered inside.

"Glass," frowned Jay. "Little pieces of glass. A whole case full of glass."

"That's not glass!" Cindy said excitedly. "It's diamonds!"

Jay gasped. Dexter whistled.

"No wonder Alex Baxter was so desperate!" said Cindy. "These must be worth a fortune. And we saved it for Mrs. Wellington." She stared at the sparkling stones.

Suddenly they heard the noise of a window being raised somewhere downstairs. "What if that's Alex Baxter?" hissed Jay, shutting the case hurriedly. They stared in the direction of the stairway.

The window was pushed down with a thud. Steps crossed the kitchen below.

The Spotlight detectives felt frozen in their places. There was no place to hide! Someone was running toward the back stairs.

"It's Alex Baxter!" whispered Dexter.

Cindy leaned over and whispered to Jay. He stood up suddenly and tucked the leather case under his jacket. Then he crept quietly to the front stairs.

Who Can Be Trusted?

"What was that about?" whispered Dexter.

"Just do as I do," Cindy whispered back. "I'll explain later."

The steps coming from the back stairs were louder and closer. Cindy quietly locked the mirror into place and stood in front of the door. Dexter stood next to her.

And suddenly Alex Baxter was in the hallway, facing them.

"You can't go into the closet," said Cindy. She and Dexter stood in front of the mirror, their arms stretched across it.

"Get out of my way!" Alex Baxter shouted.

He lunged toward Dexter and Cindy, reaching for Cindy's arm. He jerked her away from the door with one hand while he pushed Dexter out of the way with the other. Then he flung open the closet door and peered inside.

"I get it!" whispered Dexter. "Ready?"

He and Cindy leaped to the door, slammed it shut, and Cindy turned the key in the lock. Alex Baxter was a prisoner in the closet!

Who Can Be Trusted?

There was a muffled roar of anger. And then Alex Baxter threw his entire weight against the door.

Cindy gulped. Maybe he was strong enough to break the door down. She and Dexter leaned against it. Another shuddering crash. And then silence for a moment.

They could hear his heavy breathing. And then his voice. "What do you think you're doing? You're making a terrible, terrible mistake. You think you know the facts, but you don't!" His voice rose in anger.

"We know the whole story," said Dexter. "We went to see Mrs. Wellington. Jay's taken the case of diamonds home where they'll be safe until Jenny and Tom come for them."

"Listen to me," Alex Baxter said hoarsely. Now he put his mouth against the crack of the door. "I told you she was off her rocker. I told you!"

"But we saw Mrs. Wellington, we talked to her," said Cindy. "There isn't anything wrong with her at all. She likes living at the North Star. You lied about Jenny and Tom. They didn't sell her house."

"I can prove it!" shouted Alex Baxter. "I can prove

everything! Let me out of here and I promise to give you all the proof you need. She believes Jenny. She believes everything Jenny tells her—even Jenny's lies about me. Melanie Wellington is a mixed-up old lady."

"She didn't seem mixed up at all," said Cindy.

"Of course not," said Alex Baxter. "She lives in her own dream world. Her own fantasies. Harmless enough—except that now she has talked you into believing a lot of rubbish!"

"She's your aunt," said Cindy.

"Of course, she is," he answered impatiently. "Why do you think I've taken this so hard? Why do you think it's important to me? Because I'm her nephew and I love her! I want to protect her. I can't permit her life's savings to be stolen from her!"

"You're not a detective at all!" said Dexter.

"You mean she says I'm not," shouted Alex Baxter, angry again. "It's her word against mine. And I can prove I'm telling the truth. Let me out of here. I'll show you all my credentials."

Dexter and Cindy looked at each other.

Who Can Be Trusted?

The voice went on. "Do you realize what you've done? With your bungling you have let a fortune fall into the hands of scoundrels. A fortune that Melanie Wellington's husband spent his life gathering. It's hers! And now it's going to fall into strangers' hands. They'll find your brother tonight, don't worry. They'll get the diamonds from him. Your brother is all alone right now—just him and the diamonds. Do you think he has a prayer of keeping them from Jenny Mayflower and Tom Foster?"

Alex Baxter's voice was urgent. "Quick. There is no time to lose. They may be coming to look for him this very moment. They will have talked to Melanie Wellington. They will know you have figured out the secret of the iron dog and the key, and they will come directly to your homes to find you. They will find the boy and the diamonds. Hurry! Open this door!"

Cindy's heart pounded. What if Alex Baxter were telling the truth after all? What if Jay really was in danger?

She glanced down the hall toward a room that she had glimpsed that afternoon. The door was closed.

On an impulse she ran down the hall and opened that door. It was dark. She groped for a light switch and found one. She flicked on the light. It was the bedroom—the bedroom made up for guests. Vases of fresh flowers were on the tables. And there was a big sign—*Welcome.*

She ran back to the closet door. "I don't believe anything you say," she called through the door. "Jenny and Tom are really bringing his parents back here. There's a guest room down the hall all ready for them. Tom and Jenny told the truth and you lied!"

Alex Baxter's voice came through the door softly. "Don't be ridiculous! That room was prepared yesterday by Jenny, it's true. But not for her future-in-laws. They don't exist. She prepared the room for her brother, her brother who calls himself Tom Foster. They were successfully completing still another adventure in crime!"

Dexter pushed his glasses up on his nose. "We don't believe anything you say," he announced. But his voice was less sure. "Mrs. Wellington told us you'd try to lie your way out of anything and everything."

Who Can Be Trusted?

"Listen," pleaded Alex Baxter. "You kids meant well. You're trying, really trying, to do the right thing. I respect that. But don't you see? You're believing the wrong people! You're believing a wonderful old lady who lives in a dream world. Jenny Mayflower and Tom Foster have tricked all of you. You must believe me—you must! And hurry, if you want to save that boy from danger! They will stop at nothing—nothing! They're desperate now."

Dexter motioned to Cindy. They stepped away from the door. He whispered in her ear. "What if he's telling the truth? What if Mrs. Wellington is a mixed-up lady? Remember the Usher Rule—just because we like her doesn't mean she's telling the truth."

Cindy bit her lip. "I don't know who or what to believe anymore. This is scary. But I know he's lying. I know it, I know it, I know it."

"You don't know it. You feel it," Dexter replied. "And I don't feel a thing anymore. I'm numb."

Alex Baxter called from the closet. "Hurry. Unlock this door. I won't bring charges against you. You meant well. That will count a lot. Now hurry!"

Cindy and Dexter looked at each other. How could they believe him? How could they *not* believe him?

Suddenly they heard shouts and then voices. And other sounds. Footsteps running on the snow, pounding on the front door, and a key turning in the lock downstairs. A rush of people pushing to get inside. And Jay's voice shouting, "He's up there!" Cindy swallowed.

All at once lights were turned on and heads appeared coming up the stairway. Three figures ran toward Dexter and Cindy—Jay, Jenny, and Tom. And then right behind them were a man and a woman. Downstairs Melanie Wellington's voice was calling, "Oh, I'm missing all the excitement. Don't let anything happen until I get there." Then she was coming up the stairs and down the hall. Alex Baxter must have heard the noise too. There was a muffled oath from the closet.

CHAPTER 10
Behind the Locked Door

JAY RAN TOWARD Cindy and Dexter, who were still leaning against the closet door. "Are you all right?" he asked.

"Just barely," answered Cindy. "That man's still in the closet. He kept telling us we were wrong."

"We didn't believe him," Dexter said quickly.

"Didn't we?" asked Cindy.

"I knew I had to do something to save you," Jay said. "I ran in the house and tried to call Mrs. Wellington. No answer. I ran to the front porch. That's when I saw a car stop at the barricade."

"And Jay ran over and told us what was going on," Jenny finished. "You two were brave!"

They were all gathered together in the long hall, the Spotlighters, Mrs. Wellington, Tom and Jenny, and Tom's parents.

"More lights! More lights!" cried Melanie Wellington. "I declare, this place is like a cellar. And I've never heard so much noise."

"My, my," Mrs. Foster was saying to Tom. "You certainly are getting married with a lot happening."

"But our new daughter can manage," Mr. Foster said, and he put his arm around Jenny.

Cindy blinked her eyes. She didn't have any tears or anything. She just blinked anyway.

"It's all over now," Jay said.

"Not quite," said Cindy. "There are a lot of things we don't understand." She held up her notebook. "I've got some questions I'd like to ask."

Tom walked over to the closet door. "Alex Baxter," he called. "Would you mind answering a few questions before we call the police?"

There was a moment's silence. Then Alex Baxter said, "Police? You'll look like a fool. What are you charging me with? After all, I didn't get away with the diamonds. I admit I tried. But I didn't succeed. You can't arrest me for having big ideas. I haven't done a thing. Unless you count trying to take that doorstop. And I didn't even get away with that."

Melanie Wellington tapped on the closet door. "I'm sure if we called the police, they'd find something or other to arrest you for. But we'll let you go. On one condition. That you answer some questions."

Alex Baxter was silent. Then he said, "I will answer questions about the subject at hand. Nothing more. And I must have your solemn promise that you will then open that door and not impede my departure."

Dexter nudged Jay. "That means we won't stop him," he whispered.

"I thought that's what it meant," Jay whispered back.

"Very well," said Melanie Wellington. She turned to Cindy. "The young girl with the notebook may begin."

Cindy walked to the closet. "How did the iron dog get in the snowman?" she asked.

"I can explain," Alex Baxter began. "I was just trying to help Aunt Melanie. You see, I'd always suspected there was a secret safe in the house—"

Melanie Wellington interrupted. "My husband built the safe, really just a good hiding place, when we moved into the house. He loved secrets, and he loved diamonds. He collected diamonds, as Alex knew. And he liked to look at them, so he didn't want to put them away in a bank. After he passed away, I just left them in the safe."

Alex Baxter spoke again. "When I heard the house was going to be sold, I went to ask Aunt Melanie about the diamonds. I was going to bring them to her. All she had to do was give me the key to the safe and tell me where to find it. I *was* going to bring the diamonds to you, Aunt Melanie. I really would have."

"Of course you would have, Alex. But you'd have taken three or four of them first."

"Never!" said Alex Baxter. "Anyway, Aunt Melanie said that Jenny was going to bring her the key that afternoon. And then later when Tom's parents came, Aunt Melanie was going to come over to the house with them and open the secret safe."

Jenny interrupted now. "I didn't know a thing about a key! When Alex Baxter came over to the house, I couldn't imagine what he wanted."

Behind the Locked Door

"There was no need for you to know where the key was," Mrs. Wellington said. "I wanted to surprise you by letting you choose a diamond as a wedding gift."

Alex Baxter groaned. "To a perfect stranger!"

"She is not a stranger, Alex. She is a lovely friend and a wonderful girl. And I've given you plenty, goodness knows. You just want more and more, Alex. You're never satisfied."

There was a silence. Then Alex Baxter continued. "Well, anyway, Aunt Melanie said that Jenny was going to bring the key. So I went over to get it. I was going to bring it to Aunt Melanie myself."

"You were going to do no such thing, Alex, and you know it," said Melanie Wellington. "You were going to get the key from Jenny and then try to find the secret safe."

Alex Baxter cleared his throat. "When I got there yesterday and asked Jenny for the key, she was just leaving the house. She said she didn't know a thing about a key. She said she was only supposed to take the iron dog over, that was all. She didn't know why Aunt Melanie wanted the iron dog, but she was going to bring it over. So of course I knew the key was in the dog."

He cleared his throat again, then continued. "When Jenny went upstairs, I took the iron dog out of its box and put an old vase in its place. I picked up the box and the dog and called to Jenny that I'd meet her on the porch. I just had time to hide the dog behind a bush and get back to the porch to meet Jenny and hand her the box. She walked toward her car, but I pretended I wanted to check something at the back of the house. I picked up the iron dog and hid it under my coat. Imagine my horror when I saw Jenny coming back to the house!"

"I'd forgotten my car keys," explained Jenny. "I hardly looked at Alex Baxter but he said something about the snow being just right to make snowballs. Then I saw snow on his coat. He began to roll a big snowball and that seemed funny—but he always does funny things that don't make sense."

Alex sounded hurt when he continued. "It was a good idea. I rolled the dog into the snowball and set it on top of a snowman someone had started. The children were too busy to notice. Then I waved at Jenny and went to my own car."

Behind the Locked Door

Dexter turned to Tom. "But Amy and Randy were sure that *you* had helped them with the snowman, not Alex Baxter."

Tom frowned and then smiled. "I remember now. I was going over to organize the garage for Jenny. And the kids were playing around, putting a face on the snowman. I gave them a scarf for it. And I told them

to get a carrot for the nose. We always had carrots for noses on our snowmen, remember, Dad?"

"What about the scarf?" asked Cindy. "You told Jenny you'd lost it a long time ago."

"Oh, that," said Tom, blushing. "An old girlfriend had knit that scarf for me. Jenny was always jealous of that, weren't you, Jen?"

"Well, I can't knit," said Jenny. "And every time you wore it I thought you were thinking about that other girl."

"Silly," said Tom. "Anyway, I told Jenny I'd lost it a long time ago so she wouldn't fuss about it. And then when I was on the way over to clean up the garage I realized I was wearing it. So I gave it to the kids for the snowman."

"What about the mirror sunglasses?" asked Cindy. "You took them off when you saw Amy."

Torn frowned. "Did I? Oh, I remember. She had been frightened of them at first the day before, when I was helping with the snowman. It had taken me a while to show her that it was like a game—she could see herself twice in the glasses. But I didn't want to frighten her again, so I took them off when I saw her coming." Tom looked at everyone and smiled.

"I don't like those glasses either," said Jenny. "I like to see your eyes."

Cindy made a couple of checks in her notebook and wrote a few words. "Then it was Alex Baxter who put the iron dog in the snowman and Alex Baxter who came back for it."

"Please don't talk about me as if I were deaf," said Alex Baxter. "Just because I'm in this closet doesn't mean I'm not here. Yes, I came back in disguise to get the doorstop when I thought everyone was in bed. There was a whole row of snowmen! I didn't know which was the right one. I started to smash the snowmen, but I heard a car. Then someone passed, walking a dog. I decided to go away and come back later."

"We saw you leave," Jay said.

Alex Baxter ignored that. "When I did come back, the iron dog was gone! I thought Jenny must have guessed where I'd hidden the doorstop and found it."

"It was us, we found it," said Dexter.

Alex Baxter's voice rose in anger. "You little—you little whippersnappers!"

Cindy wrote the word *whippersnappers* in her notebook. Then she looked at her notes. "Tell about when I met you," she said. "Why were you hiding in your car?"

"I had reason to think Jenny had the iron dog in the box I saw in her car. Her car was locked, so I was waiting for her."

The Spotlighters looked at each other. They were sure Alex had planned to break into Jenny's car. But Jenny and Cindy had appeared, so he'd been quick to hide.

"But I gave the box to Tom," Cindy said. "And you saw it had nothing but the vase in it."

"Yes. Then I thought Jenny might have taken the dog upstairs after she found it in the snowman. It would have been too late to give it to Aunt Melanie. I was looking for it when you, young lady, came spying on me. So I used my detective identification to get you on my side. I told you Jenny and Tom were playing a confidence game."

"Confidence game!" snorted Melanie Wellington. "Alex!"

Alex Baxter said, "Please, Aunt Melanie. I was trying to help you. I could see the dog probably wasn't upstairs. I had a new idea. I thought Jenny had put it in the trunk of her car and was planning to take it to the North Star after she left her apartment. I had to find her car and look in the trunk. I wanted to get rid of the junior detectives."

No wonder he was in such a hurry to get us out of the way, Cindy thought.

"And did you open my car trunk?" Jenny asked.

"Well, yes, I did. But it was empty. I didn't have much time left. Of course I knew the riddle in the sampler. It is too easy. I guessed the safe was near the mirror. I came back here to—"

"To break in, but you were too late!"

"Yes! Somebody told these children where the key was and where the keyhole was."

"No," said Cindy. "We found the key. We found the keyhole for ourselves. But I have one question left. Didn't you get the message from your

127

answering service? We told the operator we had the iron dog."

There was no answer, and Mrs. Wellington unlocked the closet door.

Alex Baxter stumbled out and blinked in the hall light. In a voice they could hardly hear he muttered, "I never called in. If I had…"

"I hope you've learned a lesson, Alex," his aunt said. "A dozen lies won't do you any good."

"I've learned not to tangle with junior detectives." He tried to smile and then started for the stairs. "I won't stay for the party," he said.

Discover more
Spotlight Club Mysteries!

Why would anyone break into a bookmobile—but take nothing? Someone is looking for a secret among the stacks and it's up to the Spotlight Club to figure out the truth...

Albert Whitman & Company
albertwhitman.com